# HOT THINGS

## Angela Wilkes
## Illustrated by Stephen Cartwright

## CONTENTS

With thanks to Anne Civardi

# Surprise Baked Tomatoes

## INGREDIENTS

4 large tomatoes
4 eggs
salt and pepper
1 tablespoon chopped parsley

Oven setting: 180°C/350°F/ Gas mark 4

USE THE BIGGEST TOMATOES YOU CAN FIND FOR THIS. IF YOU ARE VERY HUNGRY COOK TWO TOMATOES EACH

Grease a shallow, ovenproof baking dish.

Cut a small slice off the top of each tomato and scoop out the pulp with a spoon. Season inside the tomatoes.

Put the tomatoes in the dish and break an egg into each one. Season the eggs and sprinkle parsley on top.

Put the tops on the tomatoes and bake them in the oven for about 20 minutes until the eggs have set.

Eat the tomatoes while they are hot with lots of crusty bread and butter.

# Welsh Rarebit

Mix the cheese, egg, mustard, Worcestershire sauce, salt and pepper together in a bowl.

Put the slices of bread under the broiler and toast them on one side only.

Spread the cheese mixture thickly over the untoasted sides of the bread and put the sliced tomato on top.

Put the toast back under the broiler until the cheese is bubbly and light brown. Put it on a warm plate and eat it right away.

3

# Omelette

(for one person)

INGREDIENTS

2 eggs
a pat of butter
salt and pepper

Omelettes are very quick to make. You can make a plain omelette or add one of the fillings below.

Break the eggs into a bowl. Add salt and pepper and beat the eggs lightly.

a little grated cheese

chopped tomato cooked in butter

a tablespoonful of chopped parsley and chives

chopped, cooked bacon or ham

4

Melt the butter in a small frying pan and swirl it round. When it foams, pour in the eggs.

When the omelette begins to set round the edges, add your filling.

Draw the edges of the omelette gently into the middle and tilt the pan to let the runny egg flow to the sides to cook.

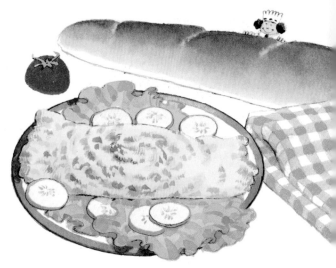

When the top of the omelette has set but is still creamy, loosen the edges and fold it over. Slip it straight on to a plate.

Eat the omelette immediately while it is hot. If there are lots of you, make an omelette for each person.

5

# Leek and Tomato Soup

A good soup with bread and cheese and fruit to follow makes a meal in itself.

Peel and dice the potatoes.

Drop the tomatoes into a cup of boiling water. Leave for a minute, then fish them out.

It will now be easy to peel the skin off the tomatoes. Chop them up roughly.

Trim off the tops and roots of the leeks and peel away the tough outer layer. Cut the leeks in half lengthways and rinse them well in cold water. Slice them quite finely.

6

Gently melt the butter in a big, thick-based saucepan. Add the leeks, stir them and cook them slowly until soft.

Add the chopped tomatoes. Stir them into the leeks and let them cook slowly until their juice starts to run.

Add the potato, salt, water and sugar. Put a lid on the pan and let the soup simmer for about 20 minutes until the vegetables are cooked.

TAKE THE PAN OFF THE HEAT. TO MAKE THE SOUP SMOOTH, PUSH IT THROUGH A SIEVE OR PUT IT IN A BLENDER, IF YOU HAVE AN ADULT TO HELP YOU

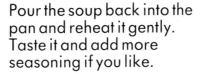

Pour the soup back into the pan and reheat it gently. Taste it and add more seasoning if you like.

Stir the cream into the soup and serve it at once.

7

# French Toast

Not all hot things take a long time to cook. Some of the nicest things are very quick to make – like french toast. You can make it for breakfast or for a snack.

INGREDIENTS
4 thick slices of
white bread with the
crusts cut off

4 eggs
4 tablespoons butter
2 tablespoons oil
salt and pepper

Break the eggs into a dish and beat them well. Season with salt and pepper.

Take care

Heat the butter and oil in a frying pan. It should be hot but not smoking.

Dip the slices of bread in the egg. Let any extra egg drain back into the dish.

Fry the slices of bread on both sides until they are crisp and golden brown. Eat french toast while it is hot with sugar sprinkled on top.

# Stuffed Baked Potatoes

Oven setting: 200°C/400°F/
Gas mark 6

Prick the potatoes with a
fork. Put them on a baking
tray. Bake for 1-1½ hours.

Push a skewer through the
biggest potato. If it is soft, it is
cooked.

When the potatoes are
cooked, cut them in half
lengthways and scoop out
the middles.

Mash the potato in a bowl.
Add the rest of the
ingredients and mix
everything together well.

Fill the potato skins with the
mixture and bake them for
another 15 minutes. Decorate
with parsley.

# Fish in Breadcrumbs

## INGREDIENTS

8 fillets of fish
4 tablespoons breadcrumbs
1 tablespoon chopped parsley
1 tablespoon chopped chives
2 eggs
1 tablespoon cooking oil
grated rind of a small lemon

Beat the eggs in a shallow dish. Season them. Mix the breadcrumbs, herbs and lemon rind together in another shallow dish.

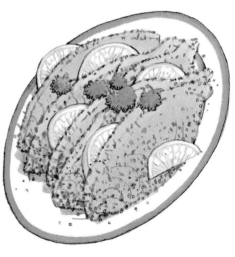

Pat the fillets of fish dry on paper towels. Dip them in the beaten egg, then in the breadcrumbs, until evenly coated all over.

Heat the oil in a big frying pan. Fry the fillets for about 3 minutes on each side until golden brown.

Take them out of the pan and drain them well on crumpled paper towel.

Serve the fish with wedges of lemon, boiled potatoes and green salad.

# Cheesy Zucchini

## INGREDIENTS

1 kg (2lb) zucchini
3 eggs
275 ml (½ pint) cream
¾ cup grated cheese
salt and black pepper
a pinch of nutmeg

Oven setting: 200°C/400°F/
Gas mark 6
Grease a shallow, ovenproof
baking dish.

Wash and slice the zucchini.
Cook in boiling, salted water
for 3-4 minutes, then drain.

Beat the eggs and cream
together in a bowl. Add the
salt, pepper and nutmeg.

YOU CAN EAT THIS WITH MEAT OR AS A MEAL IN ITSELF

Spread the zucchini into the baking dish.
Pour the egg mixture over them and
sprinkle the grated cheese on top.

Bake the zucchini for about 20 minutes,
until the egg mixture has set and the cheese
is golden brown and bubbly.

# Bacon and Potato Hotpot

## INGREDIENTS

4 big onions
4 big potatoes
250g (8oz) bacon
1½ cups milk
6 tablespoons all
     purpose flour
3 tablespoons butter
salt and pepper

Oven setting: 180°C/350°F/
Gas mark 4

Gently melt the butter in a saucepan. Add the flour and stir until it bubbles.

Let the mixture cook for a minute, then take the pan off the heat and stir in the milk, a little at a time.

THIS PAGE SHOWS YOU HOW TO MAKE A WHITE SAUCE. YOU MAKE IT BEFORE YOU START THE HOTPOT, THEN POUR IT OVER THE TOP

Put the pan back on the heat. As the sauce gets hot it will thicken. Keep stirring it so that it does not go lumpy. When the sauce boils, turn the heat down and let it simmer until thick and creamy. Season and take it off the heat.

Now prepare everything else.

Peel and slice the potatoes and put them in cold water.

Peel the onions and chop them as finely as you can.

Cut the rind off the bacon. Chop it into small pieces.

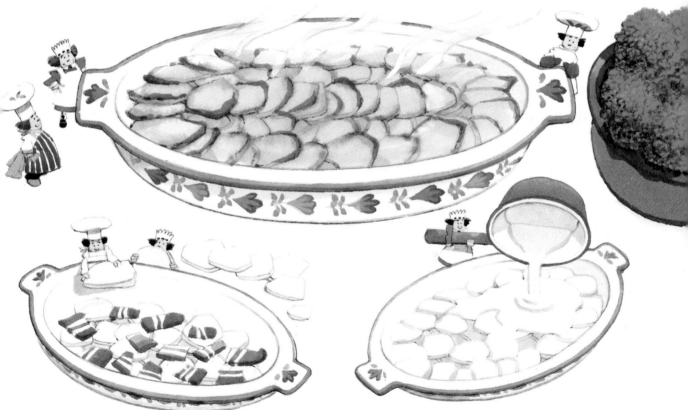

Grease an ovenproof dish and put in layers of potatoes, onions and bacon. Season each layer with salt and pepper. Repeat the layers, finishing with a layer of potatoes.

Pour the sauce on top and put the hotpot in the center of the oven. Bake it for about 1½ hours. Move it to the top shelf for the last 20 minutes so that it browns.

13

# Hamburgers

Mix the beef, onion, egg, salt and pepper together in a bowl. Cut the buns in half and toast the cut sides.

Divide the mixture into four portions and shape each of them into a hamburger.

Brush them with oil. Broil them under a high heat for 6-10 minutes on each side.

Put each hamburger in a bun. You can add slices of cheese to them if you like, or lettuce, sliced tomato and mayonnaise.

EAT YOUR HAMBURGER WITH A BAKED POTATO, RELISHES AND TOMATO KETCHUP

14

# Pork Chops with Apple

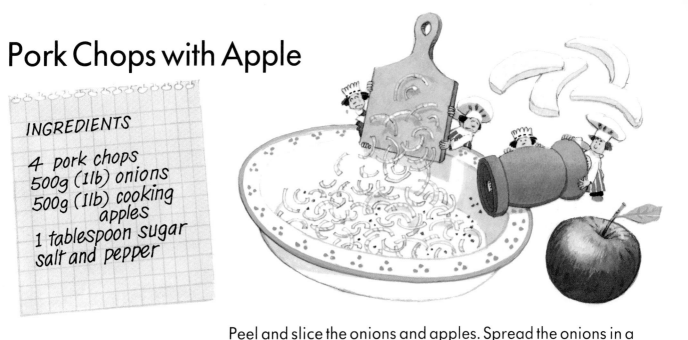

**INGREDIENTS**

4 pork chops
500g (1lb) onions
500g (1lb) cooking
apples
1 tablespoon sugar
salt and pepper

Oven setting: 180°C/350°F/
Gas Mark 4

Peel and slice the onions and apples. Spread the onions in a casserole dish. Add salt and pepper, then cover them with half the sliced apple and sprinkle with sugar.

Put the pork chops in next. Add salt and pepper, then the rest of the apple and put a few dots of butter on top.

Put the lid on the casserole and bake the pork for 1-1½ hours until tender. Serve it with potatoes and a green vegetable.

# Cheese Soufflé

A soufflé looks like a masterpiece but is surprisingly easy to make. 'Soufflé' means 'puffed up' in French. The soufflé puffs up and becomes lighter as it cooks because it contains whisked egg white, which has a lot of air in it.

INGREDIENTS
White sauce made from:

1½ cups milk
2 tablespoons butter
¼ cup all purpose flour
3 large eggs
¾ cup grated cheese
salt and pepper
a pinch of nutmeg

Grease a 1½ pint (850ml) soufflé dish or pie dish.

## Handy Tips

Use eggs that are at room temperature.

Stop whisking the egg whites as soon as they stand up in peaks.

Do not beat the mixture once you have folded in the egg whites.

Move one shelf to the center of the oven and take out the shelves above it. Oven setting: 190°C/375°F/Gas mark 5.

A soufflé starts to sink as soon as you take it out of the oven, so eat it right away. Serve it with green salad.

Separate the egg whites from the yolks. Crack each egg in turn over a bowl and slide the yolk from one half of the shell to the other. The

white will slip into the bowl. Tip the yolk into another bowl. Beat the yolks together.

Make a white sauce (see page 12). Stir in the nutmeg, grated cheese and egg yolks.

Whisk the egg whites until they form soft peaks. Stir a tablespoonful of them into the sauce, then fold in the rest. Do not beat the mixture or it will not rise.

Pour the mixture into the soufflé dish. Put it in the oven and bake it for 30-35 minutes until it is puffy and golden brown. Do not open the oven door until then.

# Spaghetti Bolognese

The important thing to remember about cooking spaghetti is not to overcook it. It should be soft but still have a bit of 'bite' to it. Bolognese sauce is a meat and tomato sauce.

Crush the garlic.
Chop the onions.

Take the rind off the bacon and chop it up.

Heat the oil in a big frying pan. Fry the garlic and onion gently until soft. Add the bacon and then the meat. Break it up with a fork and fry it, turning it to brown it evenly.

Add the tomatoes, tomato paste, salt and basil. Stir well, put a lid on the pan and simmer for 20 minutes.

Heat some water in a big pan. Add salt and a teaspoon of oil to it (this stops the spaghetti sticking together).

When the water boils, put the spaghetti in. Push it gently into the pan. It will slide down as the ends soften.

Cook the spaghetti for 8-10 minutes until soft but not soggy. Then drain it well in a colander over the sink.

Put the spaghetti in a warm dish and pour the meat sauce on top. Mix it all together.

Serve the spaghetti with grated cheese to sprinkle on top and a green salad.

# Perfect Rice

## INGREDIENTS

1½ cups rice
1½ cups boiling water
1 tablespoon oil
salt

Follow this recipe and you will have perfectly cooked fluffy rice every time.

Heat the oil in a saucepan. Add the rice, stir well and cook gently for a few minutes until it is transparent.

Add the water and salt. Put a lid on the pan and let the rice simmer. Do not stir it while it is cooking.

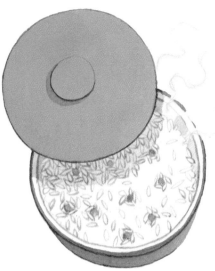

After 15 minutes (40 if using brown rice) look at the rice. It should have absorbed all the water in the pan.

Bite a few grains to test if done. They should be tender. If still hard, add water and cook the rice a bit longer.

When the rice is done, pile it into a warm serving dish and fluff it up with a fork.

# Risotto

MAKE THIS SAUCE WHILE YOU COOK THE RICE, THEN STIR IT INTO THE RICE TO MAKE A RISOTTO

## INGREDIENTS

1½ cups cooked rice
1 red pepper
1 cup sliced mushrooms
2 tablespoons tomato paste
2 onions
2 tablespoons oil
6 slices bacon
4 tomatoes
125g (4oz) peas

Skin the tomatoes (see page 6) and chop them up. Wash and slice the mushrooms. Peel and chop the onions. Core the pepper, and cut it into shreds. Cut the rind off the bacon and chop it up finely.

Heat the oil in a saucepan and cook the onion and bacon until the onion is soft. Add the other vegetables and tomato paste. Stir well, then put a lid on the pan and let the vegetables cook slowly in their juices for 15-20 minutes.

Mix the rice and vegetables together in a saucepan, heat them up and then serve the risotto in a warm dish.

# Chicken with Lemon

## INGREDIENTS

4 skinned chicken breasts

juice of half a lemon

juice of a big orange

1 tablespoon soy sauce

butter

salt and pepper

honey

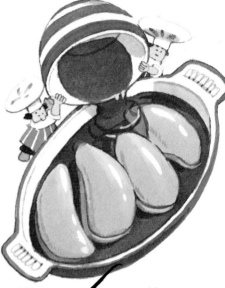

Oven setting: 150°C/300°F/
Gas mark 2
Grease a shallow baking dish.

Rub a spoonful of honey into each chicken piece and lay them in the baking dish.

Mix the orange and lemon juice and soy sauce together. Season and pour over the chicken.

SERVE THE CHICKEN WITH THE SAUCE POURED OVER IT. EAT IT WITH RICE

Cover the baking dish with tinfoil and bake the chicken for about 40 minutes.

Push a skewer into the chicken to test if it is cooked. No pink juice should run out.

22

# Kebabs

## INGREDIENTS

500g (1lb) boned lamb
4 tomatoes
1 big onion
8 small mushrooms
metal skewers

For the marinade
6 tablespoons oil
juice of 1 lemon
salt and pepper
pinch of mixed herbs

SOAK THE MEAT IN THIS SAUCE FOR A FEW HOURS BEFORE YOU MAKE THE KEBABS TO MAKE IT TENDER

Cut the lamb into cubes. Put it in a bowl. Mix the lemon, oil, salt, pepper and herbs together. Pour over the meat.

Peel the onion. Cut it into quarters, then separate the layers. Cut the tomatoes into quarters. Wash the mushrooms.

Drain the meat, then push everything together tightly on to the skewers. Be careful of the sharp points.

Put on oven mitts and broil the kebabs for about 10 minutes. Turn them from time to time so they cook all over. They are done when the meat is brown on the outside but still juicy in the middle. Serve the kebabs with rice and salad.

23

# Preparing Vegetables

Wash vegetables quickly but well in cold water. Do not soak them for too long. If they are gritty, scrub them clean with a brush.

Peel carrots and potatoes if they are big. Little, new ones need only be washed or scraped with a knife. Cut tough stalks, wilted leaves, tops and tails off green vegetables, then chop or slice them as in the picture.

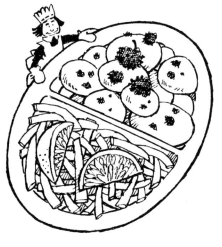

Boil a little salted water in a pan. Cook the vegetables with the lid on the pan until tender but still a bit crunchy. Do not overcook them.

Stick a skewer into vegetables to test if they are done. Then tip them into a colander over a sink and drain them well.

Serve vegetables hot, tossed in butter, salt and pepper. You can garnish them with chopped parsley, sprigs of parsley or wedges of lemon.

# SWEET THINGS

## CONTENTS

# Granola

**INGREDIENTS**

1 cup oatmeal
1 tablespoon wheat-germ
1/3 cup raisins
1/2 cup chopped nuts
2 apples
2 small cartons natural yogurt
honey or brown sugar

Mix the oats, wheatgerm, raisins, nuts and yogurt together in a big bowl. Peel, core and grate the apples, then stir them quickly into the granola so they do not go brown.

You can make a bigger amount of granola and keep it in a storage jar. Spoon it into bowls and add the apple and yogurt in the morning.

Add what you like to your granola – milk, a teaspoon of honey or some brown sugar.

You can try sliced banana with it or strawberries. Peaches taste good too.

# Banana and Honey Whip

INGREDIENTS

4 ripe bananas
small carton
    whipping cream
1½ small cartons
    plain yogurt
2 tablespoons
    honey
a handful of flaked
    almonds
a squeeze of lemon
    juice

Whip the cream in a bowl until it is light and fluffy.

Peel and slice the bananas into another bowl. Mash them with a fork.

Stir the yogurt, honey and lemon juice into the banana.

Fold in the whipped cream. Spoon into serving dishes and sprinkle almonds on top.

THIS IS MY FAVORITE DESSERT!

# Raisin Flapjacks

INGREDIENTS
2 cups oatmeal
½ cup butter
¼ cup raw cane sugar
1 tablespoon corn
        syrup
½ cup raisins

Take the pan off the heat. Add the oats and raisins to the mixture and stir everything together well.

Oven setting: 180°C/350°F/ Gas mark 4
Grease a shallow, oblong pan 18×28cm (7×11 inches).

Melt the butter, sugar and syrup together over a very low heat. Stir them together with a wooden spoon.

Pour the mixture into the baking pan and press it down. Bake for 20 minutes.

Cut the flapjacks into squares. When they are cool take them out of the baking pan. Store them in a biscuit box.

# Chocolate Brownies

## INGREDIENTS
1 cup butter
4 squares semi-sweet chocolate
1 cup sugar
2 beaten eggs
1 cup all purpose flour
½ teaspoon baking powder
1 cup chopped walnuts
a pinch of salt

Oven setting: 180°C/350°F/ Gas mark 4
Grease a shallow oblong pan 18×28cm (7×11 inches).

Break the chocolate up into a bowl and add the butter. Fit the bowl over a saucepan of gently simmering water.

When the butter and chocolate have melted, take the bowl off the heat and stir in all the other ingredients.

BROWNIES ARE CRISP ON TOP AND GOOEY IN THE MIDDLE

Spread the mixture into the baking pan and put it in the oven to bake for 30 minutes.

Let the mixture cool in the pan for 10 minutes. It will sink a little bit. Then cut the brownies into squares and cool them on a wire rack. Store them in a cookie jar.

# Juicy Oranges

**INGREDIENTS**

6 oranges

1 lemon

3 tablespoons sugar

Peel 4 oranges and cut off all the pith. Slice them and take out the seeds.

Grate all the peel off the lemon. Squeeze out the juice of half the lemon.

CHILLING THE ORANGES BRINGS OUT THEIR FULL FLAVOR

Put the sliced oranges in a dish and sprinkle the sugar and lemon peel over them. Squeeze out the juice of the other two oranges and pour that and the lemon juice over the oranges. Mix them gently and put them in the refrigerator to chill.

# Pear Pie

INGREDIENTS

5 pears
½ cup butter
1 cup flour
½ cup sugar
3 eggs
a pinch of salt
a few drops vanilla

Oven setting: 180°C/350°F/
Gas mark 4
Grease an ovenproof pie pan.

Melt the butter in a saucepan
over a low heat.

Beat the eggs and sugar
together. Stir in the butter,
then the flour, a little at a
time. Add the vanilla.

Peel the pears and cut them
into quarters. Take out the
cores and seeds.

Pour a little mixture into the
dish. Put in the pears, then the
rest of the mixture.

Bake the pie for 45 minutes
to an hour until it is puffy and
golden brown.

31

# Apple Crumble

**INGREDIENTS**
1 kg (2lb) cooking apples
¼ cup soft brown sugar
½ teaspoon cinnamon
3 tablespoons orange juice

FOR THE CRUMBLE
1½ cups all purpose flour
¼ cup sugar
6 tablespoons butter
a pinch of salt

Oven setting: 200°C/400°F/
Gas mark 6

YOU CAN MAKE A CRUMBLE WITH ANY FRUIT YOU LIKE. TRY PLUMS, RASPBERRIES OR BLACKCURRANTS

Peel the apples.

Cut them in half, cut out the cores and slice them.

Cook them in a saucepan with the orange juice, spice and half the sugar until soft.

Pour the cooked apples into a 2 pint (1 litre) baking dish and spread them out evenly.

32

# Making the crumble

Sift the flour and salt into a mixing bowl. Add the butter and cut into small pieces with a knife.

Rub the butter into the flour with your fingertips. Keep lifting your hands high above the bowl. This lets air into the mixture and makes it light. Carry on until you have an even, crumbly mixture, then stir in the sugar.

Spoon the crumble over the apples in the baking dish. Spread it out with a fork but do not press it down.

Bake the crumble for 30-40 minutes until the top has browned a little. Serve it hot with cream.

# Summer Fruit Salad

**INGREDIENTS**
250g (8oz) strawberries
125g (4oz) raspberries
2 peaches
2 bananas
1 pear
1 orange
½ lemon
Sugar

LOOK AT ALL THE THINGS YOU CAN PUT IN FRUIT SALAD!

You can make a colorful, juicy salad with any of the fresh fruit that is in season.

Squeeze the juice out of the orange and lemon and pour it into a serving bowl.

Core and slice the pear and put it in the bowl. Peel the banana and slice it into the bowl. Stir the fruit in the orange and lemon juice. This stops it from turning brown.

Cut the peaches in half and take out the pits.

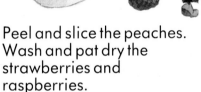

Peel and slice the peaches. Wash and pat dry the strawberries and raspberries.

Take the stalks out of the stawberries and cut big strawberries in half.

Put the peaches, strawberries and raspberries in the bowl. Sprinkle sugar over the fruit salad and gently mix it together. Put it in the refrigerator to chill for an hour or so.

You can add any of these things to a fruit salad: cherries, pineapples, apples, apricots, plums, oranges, grapes.

# Marmalade Gingerbread

## INGREDIENTS

2 cups all purpose flour
1 beaten egg
6 tablespoons butter
    or margarine
2 teaspoons ground ginger
1 teaspoon ground
        cinnamon
150g (5oz) corn syrup
250g (8oz) marmalade
2 tablespoons hot water
a pinch of salt

Oven settings: 170°C/325°F/
Gas mark 3

Grease a 20cm (8 inch)
square cake pan. Line it with
wax paper, as below.

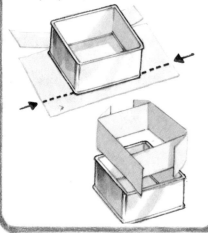

Cut up the butter. Put it in a
saucepan with the syrup.
Melt then over a low heat.

Sift the flour, ginger, salt and
cinnamon into a bowl. Make
a hollow in the center.

Slowly pour the syrup mixture into the hollow, stirring in the
flour from the sides as you do so. Add the marmalade, egg
and water and mix everything together.

The mixture should be soft and drop off a spoon easily. If it is stiff, add more water.

Pour the mixture into the cake pan and spread it out evenly with a knife.

Bake the cake on the center shelf of the oven for an hour.

The cake is done when it is golden brown and the center feels springy to the touch. If you push a skewer into the center of the cake it should come out clean.

Let the cake cool in the pan for 15 minutes then turn it out on to a wire cooling rack.

THE CAKE LASTS WELL IF YOU PUT IT IN A TIN BOX

# Chocolate Mousse

Break the chocolate into a bowl. Add a tablespoonful of water. Heat some water in a saucepan until simmering.

Stand the bowl over the pan. When the chocolate melts, stir it until smooth, then put it to one side to cool.

BE CAREFUL NOT TO MIX ANY EGG YOLK IN WITH THE WHITES, OR YOU WILL NOT BE ABLE TO MIX THE WHITES PROPERLY

Separate the egg whites from the yolks. To do this you need two bowls. Crack each egg over one of the bowls, then slip the yolk from one half of the shell to the other. The white will slip into the bowl below. Put the yolk in the other bowl.

Beat the egg yolks until smooth, then slowly stir them into the chocolate.

Add a pinch of salt to the egg whites and whisk them until they stand up in peaks.

Gently fold the egg whites into the chocolate mixture, using a metal spoon. Cut into the mixture and turn it over lightly until it is evenly mixed. Do *not* beat it.

Carefully pour the mousse into a serving dish and put it in the refrigerator for a few hours. When it is set, sprinkle grated chocolate on it. Serve it with cream.

# Fudge

BE VERY CAREFUL NOT TO LET THE FUDGE BOIL OVER!

Grease a baking pan 15×15 cm (6×6 inches)

**Boiling sugar is dangerous. Do not make fudge unless an adult is there to help you.**

Heat the sugar, butter and milk in a saucepan until the sugar dissolves. Bring to the boil, stirring all the time. Boil for about 30 minutes.

Drip a little fudge into a bowl of cold water. It will form a soft ball when it is done. Keep boiling and testing it until it does this.

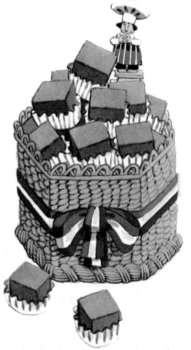

Take the saucepan off the heat, add the vanilla and beat the mixture until thick and creamy. Pour it into the pan.

Leave it to set, then cut into squares. You can make other sorts of fudge by adding cocoa, nuts or raisins.

# Meringues

INGREDIENTS

4 egg whites
1 cup sifted sugar

Oven setting: 110°C/225°F/
Gas mark ¼

Brush two baking sheets with oil and sift a little flour on top. Tap them on a table to spread the flour out evenly.

Whisk the egg whites in a big bowl until stiff. Add half the sugar, a spoonful at a time, whisking all the time.

Very gently fold the rest of the sugar into the egg whites, using a metal spoon.

Drop spoonfuls of the mixture on to the baking sheets 1-1½" apart. Shape them into rounds.

Bake the meringues for 2-2½ hours until they are set and a pale honey color. Put them on a wire rack to cool.

You can eat meringues plain or sandwich them together with whipped cream.

*See page 38 for how to separate eggs. Use the yolks to make strawberry tarts.

# Strawberry Tarts

INGREDIENTS

1½ cups sifted all
      purpose flour
6 tablespoons butter
6 tablespoons sugar
3 egg yolks, beaten
a pinch of salt
500g (1lb) strawberries
175g (6oz) strawberry
              jelly

Oven setting: 200°C/400°F/
Gas mark 6

Rub the flour, sugar, salt and butter together in a bowl until they look like breadcrumbs (see page 33).

Add the egg yolks. Mix well, then work the mixture together with your hands into a smooth ball of dough.

THE DOUGH SHOULD BE SOFT BUT NOT STICKY. ADD MORE WATER IF IT IS DRY AND MORE FLOUR IF IT IS STICKY. IF YOU PUT IT IN THE REFRIGERATOR FOR 30 MINUTES IT IS EASIER TO ROLL OUT

Roll out the pastry until quite thin. Stamp out rounds of pastry with the cutter and press them into the tins.

Prick the pastry shells and line with wax paper.
Put in dry beans or rice. This stops them puffing up.

BAKE THE PASTRY SHELLS FOR 15 MINUTES, THEN TAKE OUT THE PAPER AND BEANS. BAKE THEM FOR 5 MORE MINUTES, UNTIL LIGHT BROWN, THEN COOL THEM ON A WIRE RACK

## Making glaze

Make a glaze for the tarts by melting the strawberry jelly in a small pan over a low heat.

Wash the strawberries and take out the stalks. Cut big strawberries in half.

## Other fruit tarts

You can fill tarts with grapes, raspberries, gooseberries or apricots too.

When the pastry shells are cool, brush the insides with a thick coat of strawberry glaze. Arrange the strawberries in the shells and brush them with the glaze. It sets as it cools.

43

# Fruit Cake

## INGREDIENTS

2 cups all purpose flour
1 teaspoon baking powder
1 teaspoon mixed spice
¾ cup soft brown sugar
¾ cup butter
3 large eggs, beaten
⅔ cup currants
⅔ cup raisins
⅔ cup seedless white raisins
¼ cup glacé cherries
⅓ cup chopped peel
½ cup ground almonds
½ cup blanched almonds

Oven setting: 140°C/275°F/ Gas mark 1

IT IS EASIER TO MAKE THE CAKE IF YOU TAKE THE BUTTER AND EGGS OUT OF THE REFRIGERATOR AN HOUR BEFORE YOU START

Cut out a strip of paper long enough to go round the pan.

1

Fold back an inch all the way along it and snip it like this.

2

Beat the eggs.

Rinse and dry the glacé cherries and cut them in half.

Grease a 18-20cm (7-8 inch) round cake pan.

3

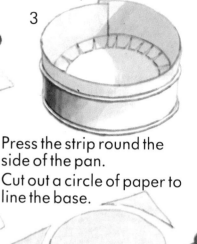

Press the strip round the side of the pan.

Cut out a circle of paper to line the base.

4

Put the butter and sugar in a mixing bowl and beat them together with a wooden spoon until they are fluffy.

Mix in the beaten egg a little at a time, then gently fold in the flour. The mixture should drop easily off a spoon.

Add a little milk to the cake mixture if it seems too stiff. Using a tablespoon, carefully fold in the dried fruit. Then gently fold in the cherries, salt, mixed spice, mixed peel and ground almonds. Do not beat the cake mixture.

Spoon the mixture into the pan and smooth it out on top. Gently arrange the almonds on top of the cake.

Bake the cake in the center of the oven for 2-2½ hours. It is done when the center feels firm and springy to the touch. If you stick a skewer in it, it should come out clean. Let the cake cool before you take it out of the pan.

# Profiteroles

Profiteroles are light, puffy little buns made of choux pastry. You make the pastry in a saucepan.

INGREDIENTS
4 tablespoons butter
½ cup + tablespoon all purpose flour
2 eggs, well beaten
⅔ cup water
4 squares chocolate
3 tablespoons water
a small carton whipping cream

Oven setting: 200°C/400°F/ Gas mark 6
Grease a baking sheet and dampen it by holding it under a cold faucet for a few seconds.

Cut up the butter and heat it in a saucepan with the water. Sift the flour on to a sheet of wax paper.

When the mixture in the pan starts to boil, take it off the heat and tip all the flour into it at once.

Beat the mixture until it is smooth and comes away from the sides of the pan. This only takes a minute.

Cool the mixture for about 5 minutes then beat in the egg a little at a time to make a thick, smooth, glossy paste.

Put teaspoons of pastry on the baking sheet and put in the oven. After 10 minutes turn the temperature up to 220°C/425°F/gas mark 7.

46

Bake for another 15-20 minutes, then peep into the oven. The buns should look puffy and golden brown.

Put them on to a wire rack. Prick a hole in the side of each one with the point of a knife to let out any steam.

Put the chocolate and water in a bowl. Heat gently over a pan of water until the chocolate melts. Stir until smooth, then put aside.

Make a hole in the side of each profiterole and fill them with a teaspoonful of whipped cream.

Pile the profiteroles on to a serving plate and pour the chocolate sauce over them.

# Handy Hints

## Mixing

Use a wooden spoon to mix ingredients together, to stir things in a pan and to add eggs or egg yolks to a mixture.

## Beating Eggs

Beat eggs with a wire whisk or fork until they are well mixed and frothy. Stand the bowl on a damp cloth to stop it from sliding about.

## Whisking Eggs

Whisk egg whites until they form soft peaks. If you whisk them for too long they go lumpy and will not fold into a mixture properly.

## Greasing a tin

Put a tiny piece of butter or margarine on some kitchen paper and rub it round the inside of the tin until it is lightly greased all over.

## Icing a cake

To spread icing easily, use a rounded knife dipped in warm water to smooth it over the top and sides of a cake.

## Looking good

Always make things look nice before you serve them. Lemon and orange butterflies and twists make good decorations for cakes and puddings.

# PARTY THINGS

## CONTENTS

# Pizza

Bread dough takes a long time to rise, so start making it 2½ hours before you want to eat the pizza. Grease two 20cm (8 inch) pie pans.

INGREDIENTS
2 cups all purpose flour
1 teaspoon salt
2 level teaspoons dried yeast
½ teaspoon sugar
75-150ml (⅛-¼ pint) warm tap water
1 medium can tomatoes
1 tablespoon tomato paste
1 teaspoon dried oregano
¾ cup grated cheese
salt and pepper

Oven setting: 230°C/450°F/Gas mark 8

Put 2 tablespoons of warm water in a pitcher and mix in the sugar and yeast. Put the mixture in a warm place for 10 minutes, until frothy.

Sift the flour and salt into a bowl. Mix in the yeast, then just enough warm water to make a soft ball of dough that leaves the bowl clean.

Put the dough on a floured table and knead it for about 5 minutes. Push it away from you with one hand, gather it into a ball, turn and repeat.

WHEN THE DOUGH IS SMOOTH AND STRETCHY, PUT IT IN A GREASED BOWL, COVER IT AND PUT IT IN A WARM PLACE FOR ABOUT AN HOUR

When it has doubled in size, take it out of the bowl and knead it for 5 more minutes. Split it into two balls and put each one in a pie pan.

Press the balls of dough out with your hands so they fill the pans. Pinch round the edges to make a border.

Drain the tomatoes and rub them through a sieve into a bowl. Stir in the tomato paste, salt and pepper.

Spread the tomato sauce over the pizzas, leaving the rims clear. Sprinkle the cheese and oregano on top.

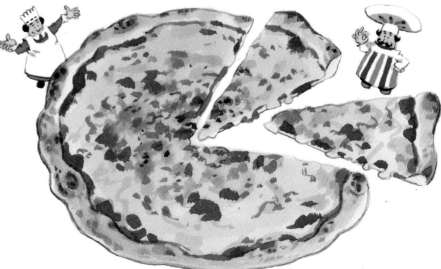

Bake the pizzas on the middle shelf of the oven for 20-30 minutes until crisp and brown round the edges.

Eat the pizza hot. Cut it into wedges and serve it with salad. You can vary the toppings by adding strips of ham or bacon, sliced mushrooms, sliced sausage, olives or anchovies.

# Quiche Lorraine

INGREDIENTS
1½ cups all purpose flour
6 tablespoons butter
        or margarine
3 tablespoons cold water
a pinch of salt

FOR THE FILLING
6 slices of bacon
275 ml (½ pint) cream
2 large eggs
salt and pepper
a pinch of nutmeg

Oven setting: 200°C/400°F/
Gas mark 6
Grease a 20cm (8 inch) pie
pan

"QUICHE" IS A FRENCH WORD FOR PIE. THE RECIPE FOR THIS BACON AND CREAM PIE COMES FROM LORRAINE IN EASTERN FRANCE

Cut up the butter. Put it in a bowl with the flour and salt. Rub them together until they look like breadcrumbs.

Sprinkle the water into the bowl. Mix the dough until it forms a soft ball that leaves the bowl clean.

IF THE DOUGH IS CRUMBLY, ADD MORE WATER; IF IT IS STICKY, ADD MORE FLOUR. SPRINKLE FLOUR ON A TABLE AND YOUR ROLLING PIN

Roll the pastry out thinly into a rough circle. Line the pan with it, prick it with a fork and trim off the edges.

52

Now make the filling. Cut the rind off the bacon. Chop the bacon up and fry it gently.

Beat the eggs and cream in a bowl and season them with salt, pepper and nutmeg.

Spread the bacon over the pastry and pour the egg mixture on top.

YOU CAN ADD LOTS OF DIFFERENT THINGS TO QUICHE—GRATED CHEESE, MUSHROOMS, LEEKS, TOMATOES OR ONIONS

Put the quiche in the oven and cook it for 30 minutes. It is done when the filling has set in the middle and is puffy and golden brown. You can eat it hot or cold. Serve it with a salad and hot French bread.

# Juicy Mixed Salad

A good salad is crunchy and colorful. Use any fresh vegetables you like and add fruits, nuts, seeds or cheese.

INGREDIENTS
½ crisp lettuce
¼ cucumber
2 tomatoes
2 sticks celery
2 carrots
1 eating apple
a handful of nuts
1 tablespoon chopped chives
1 tablespoon chopped parsley

Shred the lettuce.

Dice the cucumber.

Chop the tomatoes, celery, carrots and apple.

BASIC DRESSING
3 tablespoons oil
1 tablespoon vinegar
a pinch of mustard
salt and black pepper
a pinch of sugar

Put everything in a screwtop jar and shake it well.

DO NOT ADD THE DRESSING TOO SOON

Mix all the vegetables in a large bowl. Ten minutes before you serve the salad, pour on the dressing and toss it.

# Potato Salad

INGREDIENTS
500g (1lb) small,
white potatoes
half a bunch of spring
onions
4 tablespoons dressing
(see p. 54)
salt and pepper
1 tablespoon chopped
parsley

Scrub the potatoes and cook
them in boiling water for
10-15 minutes until tender.

Drain them well.

Clean and trim the spring
onions. Chop them finely.

When the potatoes have
cooled, chop them roughly.

Put them in a salad bowl with the onion. Pour the dressing on
the salad and mix it gently. Sprinkle the parsley on top.

# Fancy Sandwiches

You can make all sorts of sandwiches by using different kinds of bread and rolls and by making lots of different fillings. Here are some ideas to try.

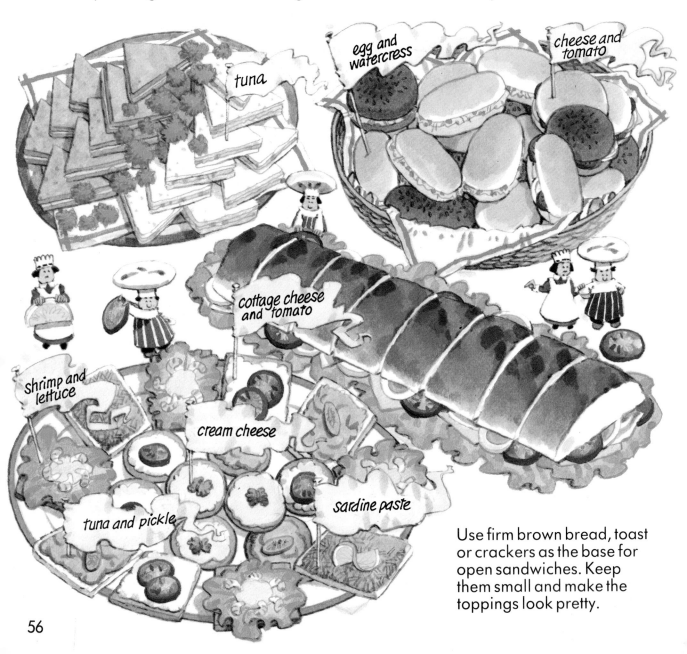

tuna

egg and watercress

cheese and tomato

cottage cheese and tomato

shrimp and lettuce

cream cheese

tuna and pickle

sardine paste

Use firm brown bread, toast or crackers as the base for open sandwiches. Keep them small and make the toppings look pretty.

## Ideas for Fillings

TRY DIFFERENT MIXTURES OF FLAVORS IN SANDWICHES AND PUT CRUNCHY THINGS WITH SMOOTH THINGS

* chopped egg and mayonnaise
* tuna fish, mayonnaise and chopped celery
* cream cheese, raisins and lettuce
* diced chicken, mayonnaise and sweetcorn
* roast beef and horseradish sauce
* grated cheese and grated carrot
* ham and cheese
* bacon, lettuce and cucumber
* flaked crab, mayonnaise and tomato
* sliced banana and honey

## Handy Hints

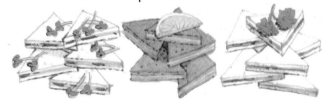

Sandwiches must be easy to eat. Cut the bread finely.

Take the butter out of the refrigerator a little while before you make the sandwiches. It makes it easier to spread.

Do not make the fillings too runny or put so much into the sandwiches that it oozes out of them.

Garnish your sandwiches with parsley and lemon to make them look pretty.

# Cheese and Herb Dip

INGREDIENTS
1½ cups cream cheese
⅔ cup cream
2 finely chopped spring onions
2 tablespoons fresh chopped parsley
2 tablespoons fresh snipped chives
2 teaspoons chopped mint
1 crushed clove garlic
a squeeze of lemon juice

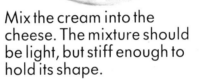

Mix the cream into the cheese. The mixture should be light, but stiff enough to hold its shape.

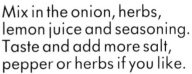

Mix in the onion, herbs, lemon juice and seasoning. Taste and add more salt, pepper or herbs if you like.

Prepare the vegetables. Peel the carrots and cucumber and trim the celery. Cut them all into finger-length sticks.

Spoon the dip into a dish and push the vegetables into it.

58

# Hot Herb Bread

INGREDIENTS

1 French loaf
6 tablespoons
    softened butter
2 crushed cloves
    garlic (if you like)
1 tablespoon chopped
    parsley
1 tablespoon snipped
    chives

Oven setting: 200°C/400°F/
Gas mark 6

Mix the butter, herbs and garlic together.

Make cuts along the loaf but do not cut right through it.

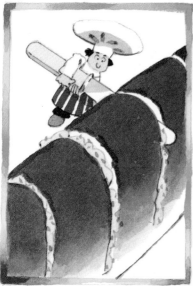

Spread both sides of each cut with herb butter.

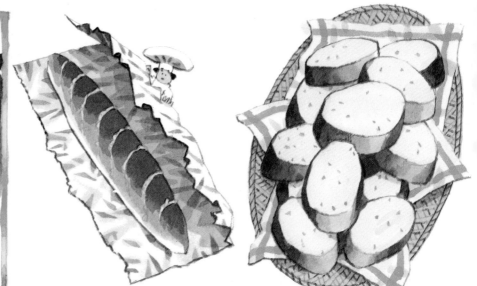

Wrap the loaf in tin foil. Bake it for 10-15 minutes.

Eat the bread hot. It tastes wonderful with salad.

59

# Stuffed Eggs

INGREDIENTS
as many eggs as you like
mayonnaise
salt and pepper
finely chopped parsley

Put the eggs in a saucepan of cold water. Bring the water to a boil, then let it simmer for 10 minutes.

THIS STOPS A BLACK RING FROM FORMING AROUND THE YOLKS!

Take the pan off the heat and put it under a cold tap. Run the cold water into it until the eggs are cool.

Tap the eggs on a hard surface to crack the shells. Peel the shells off. Cut the eggs in half lengthways.

Scoop the yolks into a bowl. Mash them up, stir in enough mayonnaise to make a stiff paste. Add salt and pepper.

Spoon the yolk mixture back into the whites of the eggs and sprinkle a little chopped parsley on top.

# Sausage Rolls

Oven setting: 220°C/435°F/
Gas mark 7
Grease a baking sheet.

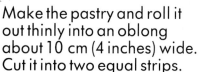

Make the pastry and roll it
out thinly into an oblong
about 10 cm (4 inches) wide.
Cut it into two equal strips.

Cut the meat in half and roll it
into two "sausages" as long
as the strips of pastry. Lay
them down the center of the
pastry strips.

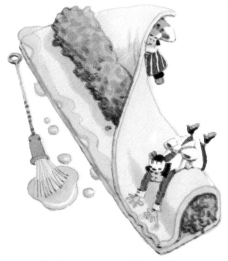

Brush the sides of the strips
with egg. Fold one side of
each strip over the sausage
meat and press the pastry
edges firmly together.

Cut the rolls into small
pieces. Brush them with
beaten egg and cut two slits
in the top of each one. Put
them on a baking sheet.

Bake them for 20-25 minutes
until golden brown.

61

# Ice Cream Sundaes

YOU CAN HAVE GREAT FUN MAKING ICE CREAM SUNDAES. YOU NEED DIFFERENT FLAVORS OF ICE CREAM, SOME SAUCES, CHOPPED NUTS, FRUIT AND GRATED CHOCOLATE. HERE ARE SOME IDEAS TO TRY—

mixed ice creams with chocolate sauce

coffee ice cream with toffee sauce

vanilla ice cream sliced banana and raspberry sauce

vanilla ice cream, pears and chocolate sauce

## CHOCOLATE SAUCE
4 squares semi-sweet chocolate
3 tablespoons water

Break the chocolate into pieces and put it in a small bowl with the water.

Stand this over a pan of simmering water until the chocolate melts. Stir well.

## RASPBERRY SAUCE
250g (8oz) raspberries
4 tablespoons sugar

Wash the raspberries then press them through a nylon sieve into a bowl.

Stir in the sugar a spoonful at a time and beat well until the sugar has dissolved.

## TOFFEE SAUCE
30g (1oz) butter or margarine
90g (3oz) brown sugar
2 tablespoons corn syrup
4 tablespoons cream

Put the butter, sugar and syrup in a small pan. Heat them gently until they melt.

Add the cream and stir everything together. Serve the sauce hot or cold.

# Pancakes

INGREDIENTS
2 cups all purpose flour
a pinch of salt
2½ cups milk and
    water, mixed
2 eggs
1 tablespoon
    melted butter

Sift the flour and salt into a big mixing bowl. Hold the sieve up high so that lots of air gets into the flour.

Make a hollow in the flour and break in the eggs. Whisk them, drawing in some flour from the sides.

IF YOU CAN, LEAVE THE MIXTURE, OR BATTER, AS IT IS NOW CALLED, TO STAND FOR AN HOUR OR SO

Add the water and milk a little at a time. Keep whisking and drawing in the flour until everything is mixed together.

Add the melted butter. Beat the mixture until it is smooth and just thick enough to coat a wooden spoon.

Melt a little butter in a small frying pan and swirl it around. Pour half a cup of batter into the frying pan.

Quickly tilt the pan in all directions until a thin film of batter covers the base.

Cook the pancake until bubbles appear and the edges turn brown. Flip it over and cook it on the other side.

Slip it on to a warm plate, sprinkle it with lemon juice and sugar and roll it up. Then start on the next one.

Eat pancakes while they are hot. When you have a party it is fun to pass them to your friends as you make them. You can spread pancakes with warmed jam or honey if you like.

# Lemon Cheesecake

INGREDIENTS

175g (6oz) ginger snaps

5 tablespoons butter

1 cup cream cheese

a small can evaporated milk

1 lemon

1 tablespoon sugar

Grease a 20cm (8 inch) pie pan well.

Break the ginger snaps into a plastic bag and crush them into fine crumbs with a rolling pin.

Melt the butter in a saucepan over a low heat. Add the crumbs and stir well.

Press the mixture evenly into the pie pan. Put it in the refrigerator. It hardens as it chills.

Grate the lemon rind. Then cut the lemon in half and squeeze out all the juice.

THE LEMON JUICE MAKES THE MIXTURE THICKER

Put the cream cheese in a big bowl and beat it with a wooden spoon to make it soft. Add the evaporated milk a little at a time, beating all the while to make a smooth mixture.

Quickly stir in the sugar, lemon rind and juice.

When the mixture is smooth, pour it over the cookie base. Level it with a knife.

Cover the cheesecake with foil and put it in the refrigerator to chill for at least three hours. When it has set, decorate it with grated chocolate or twists of lemon peel.

# Frosted Spice Cookies

**INGREDIENTS**
2 cups all purpose flour
½ cup butter
½ cup brown sugar
1 small beaten egg
2 teaspoons mixed spice
pinch of salt
½ cup confectioner's sugar
1-2 table-spoons hot water
food coloring

Oven setting: 190°C/375°F/
Gas mark 5
Grease two baking trays.

Beat the butter and sugar together until fluffy. Beat in the egg a little at a time.

Sift in the flour, salt and spice. Mix everything well to make a ball of firm dough.

Sprinkle some flour on a table and a rolling pin, then roll the dough out until it is about ½cm (¼ inch) thick.

Cut the dough into shapes. Gather up any dough left over, roll it out again and cut out more shapes.

Put the cookies on the trays. Bake them on a high shelf in the oven for about 15 minutes, until light brown.

Put the cookies on a wire rack to cool. Mix the confectioner's sugar and hot water together in a bowl until smooth.

Spoon the frosting into two or three cups and add a drop of different food coloring to each one. Leave some white.

When the cookies are cool, spoon half a teaspoon of frosting on to each one and spread it out evenly.

Before the frosting sets, decorate the cookies with silver balls or anything else you like.

# Special Chocolate Cake

INGREDIENTS
1 cup (6oz) chocolate
3/4 cup soft butter
3/4 cup sugar
4 beaten egg yolks
4 egg whites
3/4 cup ground almonds
3/4 cup all purpose flour

CHOCOLATE FUDGE FROSTING
6 tablespoons sugar
3 tablespoons butter or
                    margarine
4 squares chocolate
75ml (3 fl.oz)
        evaporated milk

Oven setting: 180°C/350°F/
Gas Mark 4

Break the chocolate into a bowl. Stand it over a pan of simmering water until the chocolate melts. Stir well.

Cream the butter and sugar until fluffy. Beat in the egg yolks, little by little. Stir in the chocolate and almonds. Grease two 20 cm (8 inch) cake pans.

Whisk the egg whites in a big bowl until they form soft peaks. Do not go on beating them or they will collapse.

Gently fold some egg white, then some flour into the cake mixture. Repeat until you have used them both up.

Spread the mixture into the cake pans. Bake for 20 minutes, until the centers of the cakes feel springy.

Leave the cakes in the pans for a few minutes, then slip a knife round the sides and turn them on to a wire rack.

WHILE THE CAKE BAKES, MAKE THE FROSTING. HEAT THE EVAPORATED MILK AND SUGAR IN A PAN. STIR AND BRING TO A BOIL, THEN LET THE SAUCE SIMMER FOR 5 MINUTES

Take the pan off the heat. Add the broken up chocolate and stir until it has melted. Do the same with the butter.

Put the frosting into the bowl. When cool, put in the refrigerator. It thickens as it cools and becomes easier to spread.

When the cake and frosting are cool, spread half the frosting on top of one cake. Put the other cake on top and spread the rest of the frosting over it.

# Cooking Things

frying pan

saucepan

wire rack

rolling pin

cutting board

mixing bowl

measuring cup

colander

cake tin

pie pan

whisks (egg beater, wire whisk)

sieve

timer

potato peeler

metal slice

ovenproof casserole

pastry brush

scales

pepper grinder

cake knife

can opener

lemon squeezer

garlic press

pastry cutters

rubber spatula

grater

kitchen scissors

baking tray

kitchen knives (1 big, 1 serrated, 1 small – all sharp)